Baby Sister

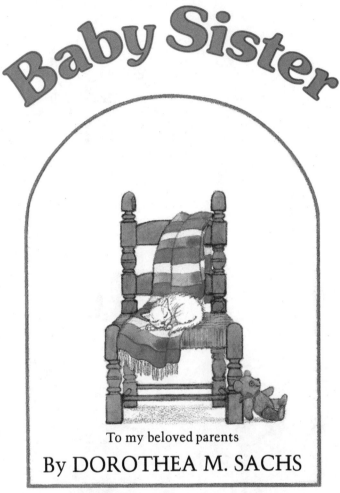

To my beloved parents

By DOROTHEA M. SACHS

Illustrated by JOY FRIEDMAN

A GOLDEN BOOK · NEW YORK
Western Publishing Company, Inc., Racine, Wisconsin 53404

Library of Congress Catalog Number: 84-72866
ISBN 0-307-02000-2/ISBN 0-307-60271-0 (lib. bdg.)
B C D E F G H I J

The sun was setting behind the mountains.
Benito put his dump truck in the big box near the
kitchen door. Then he went inside.

Mama was cooking supper. Papa would soon be home. After supper, Papa always played games with Benito. At bedtime, Mama and Papa took turns reading him stories. Mama always kissed him good night. Benito was very happy.

He was not so happy when Mama had to go away for a few days. Mama was not gone long. But when she came home, she had a tiny baby with her.

Papa said, "Benito, this is your new baby sister. Her name is Aleta."

From the start, Aleta cried. She cried when she was hungry. She cried when she was wet. She cried when she was sleepy. And sometimes she cried just so someone would hold her. She kept Mama and Papa busy...too busy to spend much time with Benito.

Now Benito had to be quiet all the time. He had to play alone in his room when the baby took a nap.

But sometimes Benito forgot to be quiet. One day he ran into the house and slammed the door.

"Mama," he shouted, "come quick! There's a bird in the apricot tree!"

Mama said, "Hush, Benito. I'll come out when Aleta falls asleep."

One evening Papa and Benito drove to the big airport. Grandma was coming for a visit.

How happy Benito was to see Grandma! Grandma hugged and kissed him.

"Benito," she said, "you've grown. You're such a big boy now, I hope the shirt I bought fits you."

They sang songs all the way home. But as soon as
Grandma saw Aleta, she seemed to forget about
Benito. And she had brought a great big box of
clothes for the baby.

The next evening Benito heard something out behind the house. It sounded like a baby crying, but much quieter.

Benito called Papa, and together they went to look. They found a small white kitten sitting all alone under a bush. Her blue eyes looked frightened. "Mew, mew, mew," she cried.

Benito asked, "Why is this cat so small?"

"She's a baby, like Aleta," Papa replied.

"Where's her mother?" Benito asked.

"Sometimes kittens get lost," said Papa.

"Please, Papa, can I keep her?" Benito asked.

"You would have to feed her and keep her warm and clean her litter box. Are you big enough to do that every day?" Papa asked.

"I think so," said Benito.

At supper that night Benito and Mama and Papa and Grandma all tried to think of names for the kitten.

Grandma said, "The kitten should be called Blanca. That means white." But Benito did not like that name.

Papa said, "Call your kitten Snowflake." But the kitten did not look like a snowflake to Benito.

"I would call her Preciosa," Mama said, "because you will learn to love her more each day. She will become precious to you."

"I will call her Preciosa," Benito said.

That first night they fed the kitten with a medicine dropper.

Then they wrapped her in a blanket they had warmed near the fire.

In a few days Preciosa was drinking her milk from a dish. Soon Mama was helping Benito open cans of cat food for her.

Each morning Preciosa awakened Benito. First she licked his face with her rough tongue. Then she nudged him with her head. Finally she poked him with her paw. She seemed to be saying, "Get up and feed me right now!"

With Preciosa meowing for her breakfast and Aleta crying for her cereal, the kitchen got very noisy.

While Preciosa ate, Benito cleaned her litter box.

When she was finished eating, Benito carefully washed her dish. Then he left fresh water in a bowl for her to drink during the day.

Benito loved Preciosa, but she *did* need a lot of care. Usually it made Benito happy to be busy caring for his kitten. But sometimes Benito got tired, just like Mama.

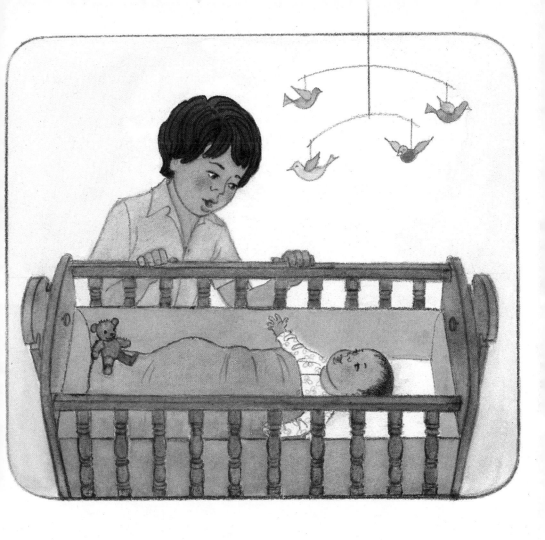

One day Mama lay down to rest. Just then Aleta started to stir. Benito went to Aleta's cradle and started to rock her very gently. Then he sang some of the songs that Mama always sang. Aleta started cooing. That was her way of singing along.

Soon she was asleep.

That afternoon Benito saw Mama struggling with a heavy basket of wet laundry. He grabbed one handle and helped carry the basket to the yard. He handed Mama the wet clothes one at a time, and she hung them on the line to dry.

Later Benito helped fold the dry clothes. He put his socks and underwear neatly in his drawer.

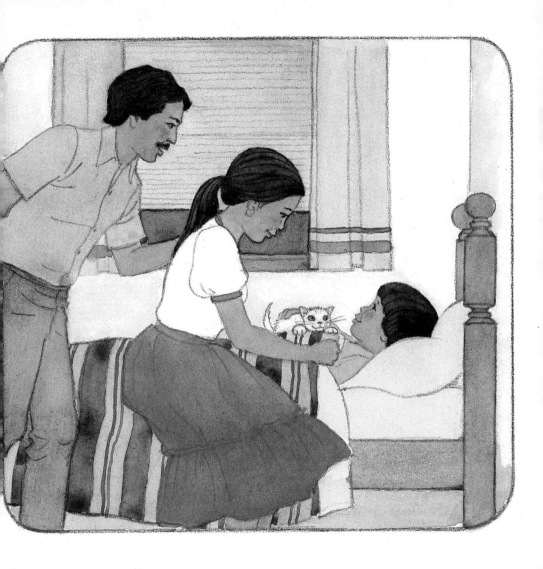

That night Mama said, "You're a wonderful boy, Benito. Thank you for helping."

Papa said, "I'm proud of you, son. You're really growing up."

Over the long winter Benito watched Preciosa grow into a plump white cat. She was learning to take care of herself. She liked to chase mice in the yard.

Aleta was growing, too. By springtime she could sit up, smile, and go for outings with the family on Sunday afternoons. Benito was allowed to push Aleta's stroller around the plaza in the center of town. Aleta looked all around and made funny sounds. Benito was proud of Aleta.

Aleta still needed a lot of care. Benito learned to feed her, give her a bottle, and play her favorite games. He liked the way she smiled whenever he was near.

Benito loved his baby sister.